DATE			
Jul 14			

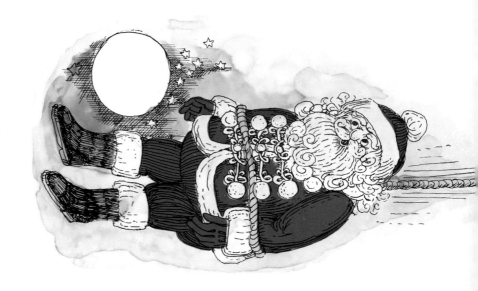

A KIDNAPPED
SANTA CLAUS

A Kidnapped Santa Claus

by
L. Frank Baum
AUTHOR OF *The Wizard of Oz*

Illustrated by Richard Rosenblum

*Foreword
by Martin Williams*

The Bobbs-Merrill Company, Inc.   Indianapolis   *New York*

THE BOBBS-MERRILL COMPANY, INC.

A SUBSIDIARY OF HOWARD W. SAMS & CO., INC.

PUBLISHERS   INDIANAPOLIS   KANSAS CITY   NEW YORK

A FOREWORD, *Mostly for Grown-ups*

L. FRANK BAUM, best known as the author of THE WIZARD OF OZ and the thirteen sequels which followed it, was also a prolific writer of children's fantasy of all kinds. Many of these tales are of very high quality. Most of them, probably because they have been eclipsed by the continuing popularity of the Oz stories, have been long neglected. A KIDNAPPED SANTA CLAUS is one of the best of those neglected tales.

Baum's use of almost medieval "morality" personifications of the Daemon antagonists in this story—the Daemons of Selfishness and Envy and Hatred and the rest—is unique in his work, and quite unusual for American literature of any kind. But the special and delightful mythology of the ryls and knooks is Baum's own, and these fairy creatures figure in many of his best non-Oz stories.

A KIDNAPPED SANTA CLAUS first appeared in the women's "service" magazine, the *Delineator*, in its Christmas issue of December 1904. After that, it was republished only once, in a rather obscure anthology of Christmas tales in 1915. It is therefore a particular pleasure to introduce this edition, handsomely presented and newly illustrated by Richard Rosenblum.

Martin Williams

A KIDNAPPED SANTA CLAUS

Santa Claus lives in the Laughing Valley, where stands the big, rambling castle in which his toys are manufactured. His workmen, selected from the ryls, knooks, pixies and fairies, live with him, and every one is as busy as can be from one year's end to another.

It is called the Laughing Valley because everything there is happy and gay. The brook chuckles to itself as it leaps rollicking between its green banks; the wind whistles merrily in the trees; the sunbeams dance lightly over the soft grass, and the violets and wild flowers look smilingly up from their green nests. To

9

laugh one needs to be happy; to be happy one needs to be content. And throughout the Laughing Valley of Santa Claus contentment reigns supreme.

On one side is the mighty Forest of Burzee. At the other side stands the huge mountain that contains the Caves of the Daemons. And between them the Valley lies smiling and peaceful.

One would think that our good old Santa Claus, who devotes his days to making children happy, would have no enemies on all the earth; and, as a matter of fact, for a long period of time he encountered nothing but love wherever he might go.

But the Daemons who live in the mountain caves grew to hate Santa Claus very much, and all for the simple reason that he made children happy.

The Caves of the Daemons are five in number. A broad pathway leads up to the first cave, which is a finely arched cavern at the foot of the mountain, the entrance being beautifully carved and

decorated. In it resides the Daemon of Selfishness. Back of this is
another cavern inhabited by the Daemon of Envy. The cave of the
Daemon of Hatred is next in order, and through this one passes
to the home of the Daemon of Malice—situated in a dark and
fearful cave in the very heart of the mountain. I do not know
what lies beyond this. Some say there are terrible pitfalls leading
to death and destruction, and this may very well be true.
However, from each one of the four caves mentioned there is a
small, narrow tunnel leading to
the fifth cave—a cozy little room
occupied by the Daemon of
Repentance. And as the rocky
floors of these passages are well
worn by the track of passing
feet, I judge that many
wanderers in the Caves of the

11

Daemons have escaped through the tunnels to the abode of the Daemon of Repentance, who is said to be a pleasant sort of fellow who gladly opens for one a little door admitting you into fresh air and sunshine again.

Well, these Daemons of the Caves, thinking they had great cause to dislike old Santa Claus, held a meeting one day to discuss the matter.

"I'm really getting lonesome," said the Daemon of Selfishness. "For Santa Claus distributes so many pretty Christmas gifts to all the children that they become happy and generous, through his example, and keep away from my cave."

"I'm having the same trouble," rejoined the Daemon of Envy. "The little ones seem quite content with Santa Claus, and there are few, indeed, that I can coax to become envious."

"And that makes it bad for me!" declared the Daemon of Hatred. "For if no children pass through the Caves of Selfishness and Envy, none can get to *my* cavern."

"Or to mine," added the Daemon of Malice.

"For my part," said the Daemon of Repentance, "it is easily seen that if children do not visit your caves they have no need to visit mine; so that I am quite as neglected as you are."

"And all because of this person they call Santa Claus!" exclaimed the Daemon of Envy. "He is simply ruining our business, and something must be done at once."

12

To this they readily agreed; but what to do was another and more difficult matter to settle. They knew that Santa Claus worked all through the year at his castle in the Laughing Valley, preparing the gifts he was to distribute on Christmas Eve; and at first they resolved to try to tempt him into their caves, that they might lead him on to the terrible pitfalls that ended in destruction.

13

So the very next day, while Santa Claus was busily at work, surrounded by his little band of assistants, the Daemon of Selfishness came to him and said:

"These toys are wonderfully bright and pretty. Why do you not keep them for yourself? It's a pity to give them to those noisy boys and fretful girls, who break and destroy them so quickly."

"Nonsense!" cried the old graybeard, his bright eyes twinkling merrily as he turned toward the tempting Daemon. "The boys and girls are never so noisy and fretful after receiving my presents, and if I can make them happy for one day in the year I am quite content."

So the Daemon went back to the others, who awaited him in their caves, and said:

"I have failed, for Santa Claus is not at all selfish."

The following day the Daemon of Envy visited Santa Claus. Said he: "The toy shops are full of playthings quite as pretty as those you are making. What a shame it is that they should interfere with your business! They make toys by machinery much quicker than you can make them by hand; and they sell them for money, while you get nothing at all for your work."

But Santa Claus refused to be envious of the toy shops.

"I can supply the little ones but once a year—on Christmas Eve," he answered; "for the children are many, and I am but one. And as my work is one of love and kindness I would be ashamed to receive money for my little gifts. But throughout all the year the children must be amused in some way, and so the toy shops are able to bring much happiness to my little friends. I like the toy shops, and am glad to see them prosper."

In spite of this second rebuff, the Daemon of Hatred thought he would try to influence Santa Claus. So the next day he entered the busy workshop and said:

"Good morning, Santa! I have bad news for you."

"Then run away, like a good fellow," answered Santa Claus. "Bad news is something that should be kept secret and never told."

"You cannot escape this, however," declared the Daemon; "for in the world are a good many who do not believe in Santa Claus, and these you are bound to hate bitterly, since they have so wronged you."

"Stuff and rubbish!" cried Santa.

"And there are others who resent your making children happy and who sneer at you and call you a foolish old rattlepate! You are quite right to hate such base slanderers, and you ought to be revenged upon them for their evil words."

"But I don't hate 'em!" exclaimed Santa Claus positively. "Such people do me no real harm, but merely render themselves and their children unhappy. Poor things! I'd much rather help them any day than injure them."

Indeed, the Daemons could not tempt old Santa Claus in any way. On the contrary, he was shrewd enough to see that their object in visiting him was to make mischief and trouble, and his cheery laughter disconcerted the evil ones and showed to them the folly of such an undertaking. So they abandoned honeyed words and determined to use force.

It is well known that no harm can come to Santa Claus while he is in the Laughing Valley, for the fairies, and ryls, and knooks all protect him. But on Christmas Eve he drives his reindeer out into the big world, carrying a sleighload of toys and pretty gifts to the children; and this was the time and the occasion when his enemies had the best chance to injure him. So the Daemons laid their plans and awaited the arrival of Christmas Eve.

19

The moon shone big and white in the sky, and the snow lay crisp and sparkling on the ground as Santa Claus cracked his whip and sped away out of the Valley into the great world beyond. The roomy sleigh was packed full with huge sacks of toys, and as the reindeer dashed onward our jolly old Santa

20

laughed and whistled and sang for very joy. For in all his merry
life this was the one day in the year when he was happiest—the
day he lovingly bestowed the treasures of his workshop upon the
little children.

It would be a busy night for him, he well knew. As he whistled

21

and shouted and cracked his whip again, he reviewed in mind all the towns and cities and farmhouses where he was expected, and figured that he had just enough presents to go around and make every child happy. The reindeer knew exactly what was expected of them, and dashed along so swiftly that their feet scarcely seemed to touch the snow-covered ground.

Suddenly a strange thing happened: a rope shot through the moonlight and a big noose that was in the end of it settled over the arms and body of Santa Claus and drew tight. Before he could resist or even cry out he was jerked from the seat of the sleigh and tumbled head foremost into a snowbank, while the

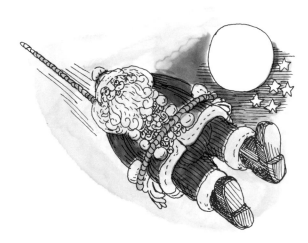

reindeer rushed onward with the load of toys and carried it quickly out of sight and sound.

Such a surprising experience confused old Santa for a moment, and when he had collected his senses he found that the wicked Daemons had

pulled him from the snowdrift
and bound him tightly with
many coils of the stout rope. And
then they carried the kidnapped
Santa Claus away to their
mountain, where they thrust the
prisoner into a secret cave and
chained him to the rocky wall so
that he could not escape.

"Ha, ha!" laughed the Daemons, rubbing their hands
together with cruel glee. "What will the children do now? How
they will cry and scold and storm when they find there are no
toys in their stockings and no gifts on their Christmas trees!
And what a lot of punishment they will receive from their
parents, and how they will flock to our Caves of Selfishness, and
Envy, and Hatred, and Malice! We have done a mighty clever
thing, we Daemons of the Caves!"

Now it so chanced that on this Christmas Eve the good Santa Claus had taken with him in his sleigh Nuter the Ryl, Peter the Knook, Kilter the Pixie, and a small fairy named Wisk—his four favorite assistants. These little people he had often found very useful in helping him to distribute his gifts to the children, and when their master was so suddenly dragged from the sleigh they were all snugly tucked underneath the seat, where the sharp wind could not reach them.

The tiny immortals knew nothing of the capture of Santa Claus until some time after he had disappeared. But finally they missed his cheery voice, and as their master always sang or whistled on his journeys, the silence warned them that something was wrong.

Little Wisk stuck out his head from underneath the seat and found Santa Claus gone and no one to direct the flight of the reindeer.

"Whoa!" he called out, and the deer obediently slackened speed and came to a halt.

Peter and Nuter and Kilter all jumped upon the seat and looked back over the track made by the sleigh. But Santa Claus had been left miles and miles behind.

"What shall we do?" asked Wisk anxiously, all the mirth and mischief banished from his wee face by this great calamity.

"We must go back at once and find our master," said Nuter the Ryl, who thought and spoke with much deliberation.

"No, no!" exclaimed Peter the Knook, who, cross and crabbed though he was, might always be depended upon in an emergency. "If we delay, or go back, there will not be time to get the toys to the children before morning; and that would grieve Santa Claus more than anything else."

25

"It is certain that some wicked creatures have captured him,"
added Kilter thoughtfully, "and their object must be to
make the children unhappy. So our first duty is to get the toys
distributed as carefully as if Santa Claus were himself
present. Afterward we can search for our master and easily
secure his freedom."

This seemed such good and sensible advice that the others at

once resolved to adopt it. So Peter the Knook called to the reindeer, and the faithful animals again sprang forward and dashed over hill and valley, through forest and plain, until they came to the houses wherein children lay sleeping and dreaming of the pretty gifts they would find on Christmas morning.

The little immortals had set themselves a difficult task, for although they had assisted Santa Claus on many of his journeys, their master had always directed and guided them and told them exactly what he wished them to do. But now they

27

had to distribute the toys according to their own judgment, and they did not understand children as well as did old Santa. So it is no wonder they made some laughable errors.

Mamie Brown, who wanted a doll, got a drum instead; and a drum is of no use to a girl who loves dolls. And Charlie Smith, who delights to romp and play out of doors, and who wanted some new rubber boots to keep his feet dry, received a sewing box filled with colored worsteds and threads and needles, which made him so provoked that he thoughtlessly called our dear Santa Claus a fraud.

Had there been many such mistakes the Daemons would have accomplished their evil purpose and made the children unhappy. But the little friends of the absent Santa Claus labored faithfully and intelligently to carry out their master's ideas, and they made fewer errors than might be expected under such unusual circumstances.

And, although they worked as swiftly as possible, day had begun to break before the toys and other presents were all

distributed; so for the first time in many years the reindeer trotted into the Laughing Valley, on their return, in broad daylight, with the brilliant sun peeping over the edge of the forest to prove they were far behind their accustomed hours.

Having put the deer in the stable, the little folk began to wonder how they might rescue their master; and they realized they must discover, first of all, what had happened to him and where he was.

31

So Wisk the Fairy transported himself to the bower of the Fairy Queen, which was located deep in the heart of the Forest of Burzee; and once there, it did not take him long to find out all about the naughty Daemons and how they had kidnapped the good Santa Claus to prevent his making children happy. The Fairy Queen also promised her assistance, and then, fortified by this powerful support, Wisk flew back to where Nuter and Peter and Kilter awaited him, and the four counseled together and laid plans to rescue their master from his enemies.

It is possible that Santa Claus was not as merry as usual during the night that succeeded his capture. For although he had faith in the judgment of his little friends he could not avoid a certain amount of worry, and an anxious look would creep at times into his kind old eyes as he thought of the disappointment that might await his dear little children. And the Daemons, who guarded him by turns, one after another, did not neglect

32

to taunt him with contemptuous words in his helpless condition.

When Christmas Day dawned the Daemon of Malice was guarding the prisoner, and his tongue was sharper than that of any of the others.

"The children are waking up, Santa!" he cried. "They are waking up to find their stockings empty! Ho, ho! How they will quarrel, and wail, and stamp their feet in anger! Our caves will be full today, old Santa! Our caves are sure to be full!"

But to this, as to other like taunts, Santa Claus answered nothing. He was much grieved by his capture, it is true; but his courage did not forsake him. And, finding that the prisoner would not reply to his jeers, the Daemon of Malice presently went away, and sent the Daemon of Repentance to take his place.

This last personage was not so disagreeable as the others. He had gentle and refined features, and his voice was soft and pleasant in tone.

"My brother Daemons do not trust me overmuch," said he, as he entered the cavern; "but it is morning, now, and the mischief is done. You cannot visit the children again for another year."

"That is true," answered Santa Claus, almost cheerfully; "Christmas Eve is past, and for the first time in centuries I have not visited my children."

"The little ones will be greatly disappointed," murmured the Daemon of Repentance, almost regretfully; "but that cannot be helped now. Their grief is likely to make the children selfish and envious and hateful, and if they come to the Caves of the Daemons today I shall get a chance to lead some of them to my Cave of Repentance."

"Do you never repent, yourself?" asked Santa Claus, curiously.

"Oh, yes, indeed," answered the Daemon. "I am even now repenting that I assisted in your capture. Of course it is too late to remedy the evil that has been done; but repentance, you know, can come only after an evil thought or deed, for in the beginning there is nothing to repent of."

"So I understand," said Santa Claus. "Those who avoid evil need never visit your cave."

"As a rule, that is true," replied the Daemon; "yet you, who have done no evil, are about to visit my cave at once; for to prove that I sincerely regret my share in your capture I am going to permit you to escape."

This speech greatly surprised the prisoner, until he reflected
that it was just what might be expected of the Daemon of
Repentance. The fellow at once busied himself untying the knots
that bound Santa Claus and unlocking the chains that fastened
him to the wall. Then he led the way through a long tunnel
until they both emerged in the Cave of Repentance.

"I hope you will forgive me," said the Daemon pleadingly.
"I am not really a bad person, you know; and I believe I
accomplish a great deal of good in the world."

With this he opened a back door that let in a flood of sunshine,
and Santa Claus sniffed the fresh air gratefully.

"I bear no malice," said he to the Daemon, in a gentle voice;
"and I am sure the world would be a dreary place without you.
So, good morning, and a Merry Christmas to you!"

With these words he stepped out to greet the bright morning,
and a moment later he was trudging along, whistling softly
to himself, on his way to his home in the Laughing Valley.

Marching over the snow toward the mountain was a vast
army, made up of the most curious creatures imaginable. There
were numberless knooks from the forest, as rough and
crooked in appearance as the gnarled branches of the trees they
ministered to. And there were dainty ryls from the fields, each
one bearing the emblem of the flower or plant it guarded.
Behind these were many ranks of pixies, gnomes and nymphs,

38

and in the rear a thousand beautiful fairies floated along in
gorgeous array.

This wonderful army was led by Wisk, Peter, Nuter, and
Kilter, who had assembled it to rescue Santa Claus from
captivity and to punish the Daemons who had dared to take
him away from his beloved children.

And, although they looked so bright and peaceful, the little
immortals were armed with powers that would be very terrible

to those who had incurred their anger. Woe to the Daemons
of the Caves if this mighty army of vengeance ever met them!

But lo! coming to meet his loyal friends appeared the
imposing form of Santa Claus, his white beard floating in the
breeze and his bright eyes sparkling with pleasure at this proof
of the love and veneration he had inspired in the hearts of the
most powerful creatures in existence.

And while they clustered around him and danced with glee at
his safe return, he gave them earnest thanks for their support.
But Wisk, and Nuter, and Peter, and Kilter, he embraced
affectionately.

40

"It is useless to pursue the Daemons," said Santa Claus
to the army. "They have their place in the world, and can never
be destroyed. But that is a great pity, nevertheless," he
continued musingly.

So the fairies, and knooks, and pixies, and ryls all escorted
the good man to his castle, and there left him to talk over
the events of the night with his little assistants.

43

Wisk had already rendered himself invisible and flown through the big world to see how the children were getting along on this bright Christmas morning; and by the time he returned, Peter had finished telling Santa Claus of how they had distributed the toys.

"We really did very well," cried the fairy, in a pleased voice; "for I found little unhappiness among the children this morning. Still, you must not get captured again, my dear master; for we might not be so fortunate another time in carrying out your ideas."

He then related the mistakes that had been made, and which  he had not discovered until his tour of inspection. And Santa Claus at once sent him with rubber boots for Charlie Smith, and a doll for Mamie Brown; so that even those two disappointed ones became happy.

As for the wicked Daemons of the Caves, they were filled with anger and chagrin when they found that their clever capture of Santa Claus had come to naught. Indeed, no one on that Christmas Day appeared to be at all selfish, or envious, or hateful. And, realizing that while the children's saint had so many powerful friends it was folly to oppose him, the Daemons never again attempted to interfere with his journeys on Christmas Eve.

THE END